AF417957

Other Books by Joseph Pluta

Voyages Across Time
Thirteen Time Travel Templates
My Best Stories
Whatever Happened to Our Dreams?
Small Town Michigan Tales: A Collection of Short Stories
Poems Inspired by Waterfalls
Before the World Lost Its Compass: Short Stories and Poems
Strolling Through an Orchard: Selected Poems
The Best Six Years of Any Life: A Memoir
Familiar Footpaths
Recollection
Twenty One Yesterdays
Two Peninsulas: More Michigan Tales
From Human Evolution to Evolutionary Economics
Human Progress Amid Resistance to Change
The Elusive Quest for Efficiency in an Inefficient World
From Adam and Eve to Adam Smith
Small Trees in the Large Forest
The Marginal Gospel
Consumers, Competition, and Corporations
The Imperfect Microscope
Markets, Merchants, and Monopolies
The Story of Economics
A Micro View of Industry (with Hilal Yilmaz)
The Art of Making Choices

WHEN LEAVES FALL

UPON THE

WINDING ROAD

JOSEPH E. PLUTA

Kindle Direct Publishing

Seattle, Washington

Front Cover: a winding road in autumn
        photo courtesy of KDP
Back Cover: South Shore interurban in Michigan City, Indiana:
        circa 1955
        photo courtesy of Pixabay

Printed in the United States of America

ISBN-9798678462343

webpage: josephepluta.com

For My Family

No One in the World is More Important To Me
Than All of You Are

*"Painting is poetry that is seen rather than felt,
and poetry is painting that is felt rather than seen."*
Leonardo da Vinci

*"If I had my life to live over again, I would have
made a rule to read some poetry and listen
to some music at least once every week."*
Charles Darwin

*"When poems stop talking about the moon and
begin to mention poverty, trade unions,
color, color lines and colonies,
someone tells the police."*
Langston Hughes

*"Poetry is life distilled...a poet is one who
distills experience...I keep telling children:
poetry comes out of life."*
Gwendolyn Brooks

*"You can't use up creativity.
The more you use, the more you have."*
Maya Angelou

*"Poetry is the shadow cast by our
streetlight imaginations."*
Lawrence Ferlinghetti

"What can be explained is not poetry."
William Butler Yeats

Author's Note:

The poems in this collection were written during a summer spent mostly indoors due to pandemic caution and oppressive global-warming-driven Texas heat. Eclectic in scope, they emphasize my love of history and geography, interest in astronomy, intrigue with the possibility of time travel, fascination with trains, preference for small town life, appreciation of humor, and recollection of personal experiences. While the initial aim was to present an optimistic tone, that has not always been possible.

It is astounding to me how ignorance, hatred, and racism have survived and reemerged in an age when people are allegedly well informed or at least when access to information is so widespread. As a father and grandfather, I am deeply distraught at the state of the world being left to the generations who will follow us.

Betterment of the human condition lurks in the mind of many creative writers as well as researchers and innovators in more technical fields. That all of us have accomplished so little in pursuit of that goal may be one of the biggest frustrations life has dealt us.

In this anthology and in previously published poetry, the debt owed to numerous accomplished poets and writers whose paths have crossed mine over the years is enormous. Especially deserving of my gratitude and respect are Thomas Lorch and Benjamin Barrett (of the University of Notre Dame), Zulfikar Ghose (of the University of Texas), Phoebe Hoffman, Julie Houy, Joe Cloonan, Michal Overhulse, and Olive Applegate (all of the Canterbury Writing Group in Carmel, California), George Klawitter (of Holy Cross College), Chip Dameron, Tony Burnett, and Evelyn Palfrey (of the Writers' League of Texas), and Bill Slaughter (of the University of North Florida).

Their poems, short stories, novels, public readings, and helpful comments have all influenced my writing and interest in many genres of literature at various times over the past half century.

Many prominent American and European poets have provided stimulating as well as entertaining companionship on quiet evenings. Those who have had the greatest impact on my desire to pursue poetic composition are Dylan Thomas, William Butler Yeats, T. S. Eliot, Herman Hesse, Langston Hughes, Vladimir Mayakovsky, Paul Klee, Kenneth Rexroth, Gwendolyn Brooks, and Maya Angelou.

In addition, although not all literary critics would agree, several popular song writers have produced lyrics that can stand on their own as poetry even without the accompanying music. Such artists as Neil Young, David Crosby, Justin Hayward, Graeme Edge, Paul McCartney, John Lennon, Bob Dylan, Jim Morrison, and Dewey Bunnell have inspired me, and no doubt others, to write poetry. There are instances when popular music has drawn upon classic poetry, in effect sending a message to an audience that may not be familiar with a work or its author. In one case, for example, the lyrics in America's 1971 hit "A Horse With No Name" beautifully borrow and set to music many of the words and images of Eliot's "The Wasteland". Other songs address meaningful topics in language less tied to specific past literature of note but equally insightful.

My sincere thanks go out to all of the above erudite sources of inspiration and creative expression.

Joseph Pluta
Austin, Texas
August 2020

Contents

Perspectives

A Lighter Side

Yesterdays

Fantasies

North American Small Towns

Gazing at the Stars

Epilogue

Perspectives

1. Not Inconsequential

soft early morning sprinkle
awakens no one...
as if nothing has changed

warblers streak from branch
to pergola perch
cardinals whistle

to each other
rock squirrels feast
on flower beds

their respective yellow red
and two tone appear the same
as when fully dry

sago palm and mountain laurel
welcome the moisture
without altering their posture

couples cuddle under covers
unaware anything
different is happening

and yet benefits
to all passive recipients
are colossal

2. Another Austin Summer

from a pleasantly cool study
views may include colorful blooms
under tall maple trees with leaves
moving gently in mild breeze

as thermometers peak at
one hundred eight with a heat
index ten degrees higher
that beauty is modified

further lessened nearby where the
homeless are sheltered only by
viaducts and tents...the blatant
menace of global warming is

more acute for some than others

3. Mass Indignation

it is an angry world
on freeways and side streets
in everyday speech
among those who make news
those who comment on it
those who are rational
and others far less so

within families and among co-workers
in the words of editorial writers
and those who write letters to the editor
where have civil discourse and mere kindness gone?
why have we become so jaded, terse and harsh?
in what distant corner of the world might we
regain a civility once commonplace?

4. A Visitor

sitting on the back deck
gazing at the fully green trees
a nondescript bird stops to rest
on the railing and stares at me
for longer than anyone would expect
neither of us speaks but somehow
communication occurs

it gets inside my head
questions my foolishness
reminds me the leaves are
not long for this world
and will soon be falling
as fall itself commences
what follows is a nod

a smirk maybe even a wink
no sound just a farewell
as it takes flight on a
southerly path
a small group of its friends
soon follows without stopping
to acknowledge me at all

5. Better Than Planned Protocol

it was a magnificent ceremony
the only music provided by the wind
there were neither candles nor hymns
no humanly created rituals
no clever words to muster feelings

of guilt or compassion or sorrow
no collection basket was passed
the few attendees could merely reach
inside their hearts to rekindle
experiences missing for some time

as the sun lowered
under thin strips of clouds
and sank into the Pacific

6. Spectacular Sight

the only thing more breathtaking
than the village of Tofino
itself is the drive across the
mountains to get there...a narrow

road passes glacier lakes, many
waterfalls and a rapidly
flowing river...light fog rolls in
almost on cue in the same spots

each trip...brisk breezes grace lookout
points during breaks to take longer
looks and panoramic photos
of wonder at its apogee

7. Jeremy

classmates made fun of him
because he was different
introverted
unfashionably dressed
perpetually silent

boys invented stories that
he had made advances
toward them
when he and his family
moved away many feigned relief

when he died in his mid thirties
some people chuckled that
it was probably AIDS
two of his former classmates
visited his widow
and two children

she confided he never
spoke about high school
and died of a rare cancer
the two young women cried
on their return trip
to their lovely home town

the history of the world is
a somber story of wars
in every written account
of major events worldwide
group aggression and violence

have dominated...dictated
the outcome of who gained power
which nations survived...prospered...failed
due to the mass carnage of strife
what creativity...talent

lies buried in countless graveyards
what human progress has been
forever lost...what potential
happiness has been replaced
by undeserved lifelong sadness?

9. The Storm

lightening only happens
when there's thunder

bridges are only conceived
when there's foresight

progress only emerges
when there's vision

culture only advances
when there's wisdom

social mores only change
when there's crisis

10. Life With Unwanted Guests

wildlife routinely trespasses
through our well maintained property
nary a day passes without

seeing deer, squirrels and raccoons
ring tailed cats, armadillos and
coyotes are less frequent yet

seldom warrant a second glance
no matter when, snakes are always
an unpleasant startling surprise

roaches, spiders, scorpions and
other crawling critters appear
when least desired or expected

wildlife routinely trespasses
through our well maintained property
or maybe we've infringed on theirs

11. We Are All African

twenty first century research by
paleontologists, archaeologists,
and other scholars of prehistory
contains conflicting claims and evidence
about *where* in Africa the human race
originated...there is little dispute,

however, that the human species began
somewhere on that vast continent before
migrations occurred to other parts of the world
will there ever be a day when everyone
realizes we are all African?

12. Contentment

brisk autumn breeze
rattles windows
fireplace flame gives
adequate warmth
bookshelves remind

of past career
infant on lap
priceless reward
for a lifetime
of exertion

13. Our Fondest Wish

when our granddaughter is the age
we are now it will be less
than a decade until the
twenty second century

we hope the world is a better
place then than it is currently
we hope her life will already

have been filled with much happiness
with substantially more to come
we hope she loves her grandchildren

as much as we love her

A Lighter Side

14. What's Next?

thanks to the techies of the world
the on/off switch has been replaced
by needless complication

soon when one enters a public
restroom the porcelain fixtures
will all be locked and a sign

will flash asking for a user
ID, password and answers to
three security questions

a second user ID and
password might be required to gain
access to the soft tissue

this would be an unfortunate
moment to be forgetful and
the techies' ultimate triumph

15. Places I've Never Been and Wish I Had

definitely
    Yosemite...Yellowstone
    Isle Royale...Vermont
    northernmost British Columbia
    aboard the Alaska Railroad
maybe
    Big Bend...southern Poland
    Cuba...Switzerland
    the Buddy Holly Museum
    the Harvard campus
long shots
    fjords of Norway
    Mt. Chimborazo
    Machu Picchu
    an orbiting space station?

16. Places I've Been and Wish I Hadn't

northwest Indiana
southern Indiana
central Indiana
rural Mississippi
most large cities
their suburbs
Mohave Desert
a convent

aboard a roller coaster
inside a long cave
in crowded airports
in a hospital operating room
in Phoenix in summer
inside a chicken coop
on a golf course
in a saddle on a horse

trapped listening to
        a long winded sermon
alongside a highway
        waiting for a tow truck
at a party honoring
        a loathsome honoree
in a cozy restaurant
        with a vocal republican

17. Places I've Been and Would Like to Revisit

moments most worthy of
reliving might include
gazing out at the Pacific
from an overlook in Tofino

looking at and listening to
Tahquamenon Falls
viewing the steep cliffs on the
northern shores of Lake Superior

hiking in Glacier National Park
riding aboard a BC Rail coach
feeling the splashing water
from Athabasca Falls

cruising in a boat on the
Columbia River Gorge
watching the waves on
the beach at Big Sur

sitting inches away from the
rushing river in Sun Valley
observing the painted
rocks near Munising

18. Places I've Never Been and Will Continue to Avoid

like the plague
    Las Vegas
    Sahara Desert
    Antarctica
    Buffalo
    a klan rally
would drive around it
    Branson
    area 51
    Siberia
    North Korea
    a snake farm
would prefer somewhere else
    a copper mine
    my attic
    a swamp
    an ice fishing contest
    a nudist colony

19. Conspicuous Waste

neither fashion
nor anti-fashion
statements interest me

clothes exist to
prevent arrest for
indecent exposure,

winter frostbite,
sunburn in august
not to create demands

to fit in, make
shrewd designers rich,
conform to norms set by....?

20. The Extreme Golfing Mindset

the true golf fanatic will play as
scheduled and ignore all distractions
neither threat of freezing weather nor
thunderstorm nor extreme heat can
discourage or postpone an outing

one elderly gent allegedly
was about to putt on the eighteenth
green when a funeral procession
approached on the street just beyond the
fairway...he immediately stopped,

laid down his club, removed his hat and
bowed in prayer...his golfing partner
was moved and asked what inspired such a
touching act...the response was that they
had been married for forty-four years

21. Trapped By Ugliness

snow capped mountain ranges,
tall waterfalls, rolling green
meadows, beaches with nearby
dunes--all exude natural

beauty...with flat prairies that
extend as far as the eye
can see, similar beauty
is far more difficult to recognize

if it is there at all...how
does one appreciate the
wonder of scorched grasslands in
Kansas, treeless areas

in Texas deserts, southern
Illinois highways, and plains
in Indiana after
the corn has been harvested?

without an extensive dose
of alcohol or other
potent stimulant, one prone
to seek awe likely does not

22. Snow Traumas

waiting at a bus stop in freezing
weather a man reflected upon
similarly troubling incidents
among which several came to mind:

walking to class when a blizzard wind
took his breath away...parking in a
snowdrift after midnight and being
unable to open the car door

getting stranded at the home of a
disastrous blind date...falling down a
flight of icy stairs into a pile
of shoveled snow...driving snowmobiles

into a snowbank and having to
walk five miles to find help...being hit
at close range by a snowball thrown by
a mischievous young boy...and getting

stranded in a bar...while that last one
was not entirely catastrophic
it was there that he made plans to
relocate to a warm weather climate

23. Forgotten But Not Gone

irrelevant, unnoticed
tolerated momentarily
profound articulation
heroic deeds
vintage attainment
negated by
senescent appearance

Yesterdays

24. Humble Beginnings?

when he could barely walk he would
dart between stalks in the cornfield
or hide behind bales of hay
his Dad would put him up on the

tractor where he would try to steer
the wheel and pretend he was
plowing a field...he would soon be
sneaking into the garden where

he would pick and eat strawberries
in one fluid motion...sometimes
he would bring a saltshaker from
the kitchen table to season

a tomato as he picked the
ripest reddest one from the tall
green plant...he would talk to his dog
and cats and sometimes even the

chickens...he would later meet
people who might think of such
beginnings as primitive
to him they were idyllic

25. The Man in the Red Brick House

it was just another farmhouse
on a narrow country road
they were all a little different
and in many ways all the same

it had a second story
and an add on back porch
a coal burning furnace in the basement
and a pot belly stove in the kitchen

where an elderly man often rested
before feeding the cows and picking eggs
when he ran his hand through his thick white hair
his thoughts were of his ailing daughter

and her red headed toddler son
the man spoke little English
but had a warm reassuring smile
his chores would soon include cooking

26. What Was She Like?

she was born in Wadowice
in the 1880s
emigrated to America
as a teenager

and was married in Chicago
she was the most loving
and most important
influence on her daughter

the great depression reminded
her of hard times in Poland
she died while hospitalized
in the 1930s

in old photos
she looks strong and kind
I know so little about her
and miss not having ever met

my Babcia

27. The Family From Tarnow

the path between Tarnow and Rzeszow
was well travelled...a horse drawn wagon trudged
along as the couple aboard observed

workers laying track...the new railroad would
pass through the two towns en route to Krakow
gas lighting was new in Tarnow...modern

water systems were still decades away
three boys accompanied their parents on
this weekend adventure to visit their

cousins... Wladyslaw, the youngest, would one
day work as a blacksmith casting molten
iron into rails….at the turn of the

century, hard times prevailed and he would
sail in steerage class to America
years later he would be my grandfather

28. Mentor to Many

in 1950s Michigan, he owned a small town drugstore
where he worked fourteen hours a day, six days a week
he gave many local teenagers their first job
and a few senior citizens their last

he expected employees to keep busy at all times
restocking shelves, cleaning counters when business was slow
he corrected those who made mistakes, never raised his voice
his laugh, helpfulness, and generosity were frequent

the lunch counter was popular for burgers and fries
nearby store owners came for mid morning coffee breaks
Sunday church going families came for full breakfasts
children came for malts, high schoolers for cokes

he was known to all simply as Karl
of his many quotes, the most memorable was
"treat all customers with the same respect and friendliness
regardless of race or age....I shouldn't even have to say that"

29. Mementos

battered signs on the wall
of a rundown wooden
building bring back memories
of an earlier time

below ads for sinclair and shell
young boys would fill bicycle tires
and wave to attendants
as they drive off to the

baseball field or continue
their paper route...the most
poignant sign is the one
that reads 19¢ per gallon

30. Insignificant?

villages in southwestern Michigan
seldom make headlines...their lists of
notable people are short..the renowned

pass through on the freeway or stop for a
night or two...beaches and relative
quiet are draws...village histories are

a mixed bag...Capone gang members were known
to stop...Guy Lombardo and musicians
of more recent vintage entertained there

the great Jesse Owens lived a quiet
life near the Lake Michigan shore
while growing up there most locals aspire

to leave...how often they return varies
the memories these small communities
generate are many as are their

virtues of kindness, friendliness and
honesty...might that be better than
                notoriety?

31. A Town of 30,000

your factories made boxcars and cough drops
your zoo housed monkeys and Polish chickens
your downtown was vibrant with retail stores
by day and movie theaters by night

your beach was lively during summers and
abandoned during snow covered winters
you seemed big for a small town at least in
the eyes of those from nearby villages

and the adjacent quiet countryside
viewing you as inconsequential and
easily dismissed, your youth often seized
the first opportunity to exit

underappreciated by many
often underestimated by all
your vitality slowly diminished
but your best lessons lasted a lifetime

32. The Barn

cows in stalls on the ground floor
milking machine ready for use
a stray chicken here and there

bales of hay up in the loft
multiple drafts everywhere
fading red paint on the outside walls

silo storing corn or other grain
visible from the quiet road
even before the farmhouse itself

33. The Neighbors

their farmhouse and barn seemed older
the two story white frame building
had a kitchen sink and hand pump
an outhouse was a hundred or

so feet downhill from the back door
there was one electric lamp in
each room one radio and no
television...furniture was

sparse and dated...crosses and framed
holy pictures filled bedroom walls
coal and firewood fed a furnace
in the year round damp cold basement

they had no tractor...only a
team of aging tired horses
implements included a plow
rake, corn planter, manure wagon

cows grazed in a fenced-in pasture
a small wheat field nearing harvest
bordered a shed where scythes were honed
a dog and five cats roamed freely

intruders including mice but
not snakes were dealt with severely
it was a humid Michigan
summer in 1948

34. Dissociated

family friends had three sons
his occasional childhood playmates
until all began high school
the three went to neighborhood
schools in the large city where
they lived...he attended public

schools in the small town near his
family farm...he went to a
state college and graduate school
then pursued academia
the three struggled through twelve grades
stayed in the neighborhoods where

they had grown up...worked in local
factories...the professor
travelled widely, taught in three
countries, did research on
twentieth century music
lost contact with childhood friends

throughout his career he was
anything but prominent or
self absorbed...he merely sought
to remain informed and enjoyed
assisting those who wished to
learn...after he retired one of

his childhood friends contacted
him...they spent a day together
and shared memories along with

recent family photos
when musicians were discussed
the friend mocked those who were gay

and stated confidently
that police violence against
black men was fabricated by
the media...he cursed Central
American immigrants
all Muslims and Koreans

their paths never crossed again

35. The Lake and the River

the river emptied into the lake
or maybe it was the other way around
the lake had a popular beach
the river was an occasional fishing hole

water in the lake was clean
no one dared swim in the river
the lake housed mostly perch and whitefish
many species inhabited the river

locals who were not anglers wondered what
kept bass and pike from entering the lake
and perch from swimming down river

in winter both bodies of water froze
that was all they had in common

36. Professor Bogle

he had a photographic memory
and was absent minded
his lectures were organized
eloquent and insightful
he used not a single note or prop
students would routinely look back

to see if he was reading from a screen
or cue cards in the back of the room
dressed in a coat and tie
he would enter the room and ask
where he left off the previous class
he would then begin as if

he were continuing in mid sentence
his knowledge of international
relations among distant countries
astounded all who listened and took notes
one day he announced there would be
an exam a week later

students spent days
in intense preparation
on exam day he entered the room
as usual and asked
where he had left off last class
after a lengthy silence

and glances at each other
one person in class reminded him
that an exam was scheduled

seemingly surprised he merely paused
before announcing there would be
twenty short answer questions

he then composed the test on site
he wrote nothing down since he had
neither pen nor paper
afterwards students looked up answers
and agreed the test was
thorough accurate and fair

37. After All Coursework Was Completed

it took more than eight years
to earn three degrees
afterwards the aspiring scholar
reflected on the courses
he had taken
some of his teachers were outstanding
some fair others quite poor

best and worst courses
soon occupied his mind
the worst were easily
dismissed with a smirk
the best were far more
difficult to ascertain
after much thought two courses emerged

the first was taken just after high school
before freshman year
officially began
it was titled simply
'how to study in college'
and its main messages were
setting priorities and

having the right attitude
the second was audited
after his third degree was conferred
it was taught by a national
award winning teacher in his field
his own teaching career would be
modeled after this master teacher

38. San Francisco to Tokyo

flying across the Pacific
can be dull, seemingly never
ending, and somewhat frightening
unexpected wind gusts may be

powerful enough to eject
unbuckled passengers from seats
after experiencing these,
sleep becomes less relaxed...it is

best not to think about how far
it is to a sturdy shoreline
to pass the time fraternizing
is inevitable although

stimulating conversation
is not guaranteed...missing those
left behind fills the weary mind
with anxious thoughts...doubts about the

wisdom of this venture emerge
finally one who has made the
trip often shouts Mt. Fuji is
now visible...descent begins

39. Northern California Saturdays

we walked almost every weekend back then
on trails above the village or not far
from the bay, there were plateaus where we would

rest and maybe have a snack of fruit, we
kept an eye on the mountain slopes above
the air was cool year round but never so

cold we stayed home, your hair was pulled back with
some tucked under your cap, our walking shoes
nearly matched although yours were more stylish

hours passed unnoticed since neither of us
was keeping time, there was nowhere we had
to be before evenings arrived, this

was our chance to enjoy each other and
plan our future, on one walk we agreed
that it was time to start our family

40. Calm

some people visit Paris
Rome Budapest Miami
Honolulu or Beijing

our trips? the wilderness of
northern Vancouver Island
Lake Louise in Alberta
the U P of Michigan
the state parks of Kentucky
ski resorts in off season
and mountains in Idaho

there were no mammoth buildings
freeways subways sprawling burbs
or overpriced restaurants

those who endured congestion
the threat of violent crime
and pollution could not have
had better times than we did

41. Lake Michigan Stonehenge

forty feet under water
near the shores of Traverse City
six large boulders appear
to form a hexagon

one of the stones has what might be
a sketch resembling a mastodon
who put these stones here and when?
or are they some random
natural formation?

hypotheses vary
the best speculation...
more than five thousand years ago
water levels were lower
and residents may have arranged
these stones for a variety
of possible purposes:

perhaps monitoring positions
of the sun to determine
length of growing seasons?
a place of worship?

originally thought to be unique
a similar structure was later found
at the bottom of Lake Huron

Fantasies

42. Moments I Wish I Could Have Witnessed

of all momentous occasions
in history how fulfilling
it would have been to have witnessed:
the look on Hitler's face after
Jesse Owens had won his fourth
Berlin Olympic gold medal

the intense expression of a
thirteen year old Joan Baez as
she sat with her aunt at a Pete
Seeger concert and tears in her
eyes not long afterward when she
attended an MLK speech

the deflated expressions of
FBI agents who shadowed
Cesar Chavez only to find
nothing indictable and the

confident smile of Benazir
Bhutto when she was introduced
as Pakistan's prime minister

43. A Lifelong Dream

he was raised in a small town
and loved its laid back lifestyle
people were friendly, helpful
accepting of newcomers
and willing to learn from them
when visiting large cities
suffocation soon surfaced

skyscrapers, traffic, crowded
sidewalks, and noise overwhelmed;
unfriendliness and anger
were too often commonplace
after college, he tried to
fit in where jobs existed
as the years passed he longed for

the simpler life of his youth
when his children grew up and
settled nearby, he embraced
their families, accepted
reluctantly limited
elbowroom even as the
days of retirement approached

44. If…….Back Then?

if you were a bootlegger
during the early years of
the great depression...not a
gangster...just someone who
delivered to speakeasies
and to families
would you have felt badly?

if you used your sizable
gains to start a legal
business that employed
dozens of people and
provided needed goods at
reasonable prices
to those who struggled
during hard times
would you have felt badly?

if you donated even
a small portion of your
profits to charity
would you have felt badly?

if repeal of prohibition
ended your bootlegging and
made your legal business
far less profitable
causing you to cease
donations to charity
would you have felt badly?

45. The Hood

houses were small old well kept
grass was well mowed in summer
snow was shoveled from driveways
and narrow sidewalks in winter

trees were trimmed infrequently
fences were mended sometimes
broken windows were replaced
promptly as were broken locks

people walked to stores and parks
but drove to churches and schools
neighbors gathered to play cards
or tell stories of younger days

parents played with their children
in back yards and on front steps
grandparents waved from porch swings
while holding infants and kittens

where was this idyllic 'hood?
in a town before freeways
shopping malls chain restaurants
and google were even conceived

46. Lonely Waterfront

the dunes stretched for miles
with nothing in sight except
gently rolling waves and
intermittent yellow green foliage
a slight breeze barely ruffled
only a few grains of sand
grey clouds passed quickly

as distant sunlight faded
a lone barefoot figure emerged
and gazed at the white caps
that now rose to new heights
inspiration would soon be plentiful
would the result be a career change
relocation plan or a popular song?

47. Delusional Mental Disorder

some teach their children to hatc those
who live on the next block because
they look different, then bow their

heads to give thanks for……….?
then rest assured they are on the
path to some vaguely defined

eternal(?) salvation; do they
actually believe
everyone they meet in their

version of a next life will
only look like them? what if
someone different somehow sneaks in?

48. If I Had a Time Machine

so many horrible past events
would merit preventing or changing
wars, plagues, homicides, slavery and

thoughtless hurtful statements top the list
it would be nice to prevent them all
if the machine were capable of

only one trip to one event, I
would journey to the precise moment
millions (billions?) of years ago when

forces that unleashed destruction of
that technologically advanced
civilization were first let loose

the pyramids as well as other
unexplained present day wonders would
no longer be unsolved mysteries

the knowledge possessed in that first great
era would not have been forever
lost...most importantly humanity

might have avoided the ultimate
catastrophe and learned how not to
repeat it in the present and near

future...or would that be asking too much?

49. A I

science fiction writers have produced
many tales of cyborgs or other
humanly created machines that

eventually take over when
they become uncontrollable
today this fear, whether rational

or not, has grown with an extreme
version hypothesizing that
alien visitors may have

seeded in humans the knowledge
to produce such greatly advanced
artificial intelligence

making alien conquest (for them)
painless...both Carl Sagan and Stephen
Hawking have discouraged efforts to

make contact with other worlds for
fear that attack and stealing of
earthly resources might be enhanced

once our existence is known to them

50. In the Year 2125

in one hundred years what common
diseases of today will have a cure?
what new diseases might be incurable?
what will universities be like?

will they exist at all? if not,
how will people learn? or will they?
how much will technology have advanced?
will it have contributed to a

higher quality of life?
or simply created more
devastating weapons?
will pollution have been conquered?

or will it have conquered us?
will the earth's resources be sufficient
to supply its ever growing
population? will racism have

disappeared? or become more pronounced?
will kindness be more common than
it is today? or not? and if not,
how serious will the consequences be?

51. Career Fantasy

looking back on different
paths a life may have taken
an alternate career choice
often arises...slow pace
does not necessarily
replace stern intensity
greater fulfillment always
does...prolonged reflection can
lead down multiple byways
after hours or days or months

imagine the creativity
that would accompany primary
responsibility for choosing
a soundtrack to fit specific scenes
in deeply thoughtful movies...hours of
listening to music from artists
of several eras...narrowing
to lyrics that complement subplots
culminating in captivating
conclusions...a more gratifying
choice does not come to mind

52. To Have Been There..........

how educational it would have been
to have heard any speech by Lincoln,
J. M. Keynes cautioning delegates at the

Versailles Conference about the overly
stringent demands placed upon a defeated
Germany, FDR and Stalin

conversing at Yalta, JFK and
Bobby discussing options during the
Cuban missile crisis, LBJ speaking

as he signed the Civil Rights Act, Robert
McNamara publicly admitting
the Vietnam War was a mistake

Barack Obama reacting when he
first heard the Affordable Care Act had
been approved by both houses of Congress

Trains

53. The Golden Spike

the quiet country road between
Three Oaks and Rolling Prairie is
crossed by a rarely traveled single track

when the elderly tourist from
Texas strolled along the rail line
he came upon a single spike that had

evidently been cast aside
when wooden ties had been replaced
today covered in gold paint it sits on

a bookshelf in his study where
he composes stories and verse
about his fascination with railroads

54. Memories of the South Shore

it was more than a train station
people would flock to its spacious
interior for warmth in winter
before reentering retail stores

down the street...its lunch counter drew
all age groups to its daily hot
meal specials, sandwiches, malts, soft drinks
its pinball machines attracted an

after school crowd...its magazines
and newspapers were often bought
by retirees who leisurely sat
on its long benches with no travel

plans of their own...ticket sales boomed
in the final minutes before
eastbound and westbound passenger cars
approached...autos on 11th street

moved aside and proceeded with
caution as the interurban
rode a single rail while drawing its
power from overhead electric

wires...when it stopped a conductor
descended the stairs to assist
those getting both off and on...now
the front doors of the building opened

wide as throngs of commuters and
those meeting them filled the entrance
...within minutes a bell rang twice to
signal the engineer who resumed

the journey...activity on
the ground soon reached a hectic pace
employees inside became more active
it was still mainly a train station

55. Unfulfilled Wish

a young boy watched the Michigan
Central steam engine reduce speed
as it passed through his home town
he noticed people inside its
passenger cars as he longed for
the day when he would be able
to ride among them

by the time he grew up
steam engines and most passenger
trains were gone...only diesel engines
pulling boxcars passed through his home town
somehow airplanes did not offer
a similar adventure

56. This Side of the Tracks

the tracks ran just beyond his back yard
people thought he was poor for having
to live so close to a loud railroad

he believed his was the luckiest
family in town...each day he would
run outside when he heard the engine

whistle...if it was a passenger
train, he would wave to those riding and
count how many waved back...if it was

a freight train he would count the cars and
wave at the man in the caboose...as
time passed, the schedule was committed

to memory and he would worry
if the train was late...there was no such
thing as loneliness when each day was

shared with so many people from so
many places although he often
wondered why the train never stopped there

57. Crossing a New Bridge

the ten year old boy loved his
electric train and saved his
allowance so he could add
new accessories to it

box cars and gondola cars
were on each year's Christmas list
he would routinely decline
offers to go to movies

with friends so he could work at
his hobby...when he entered
high school his classmates would go
to the malt shop after school

he would go to a train store
with a hopeful gaze at its
engines and red cabooses
one day he checked his savings

and made plans to buy a freight
station and diesel engine
or maybe a semaphore
or a steam locomotive

after spending more than an
hour at the train store, he put
his money in his pocket
and headed for the malt shop

58. Satisfying Work

he had a summer job working for
the Chesapeake and Ohio Railroad
when not in the caboose, he would ride

in open door boxcars and uncouple
some of them onto sidings in small yards
across Michigan and Indiana

it was satisfying work and safe
as long as jumping off and climbing
aboard occurred only at slow speeds

sometimes onlookers would jeer at him
thinking he was a hobo, older
workers would make fun of his mistakes,

fellow college students with desk jobs
would mock him and laugh at his attire
it still was satisfying work

59. A Salute to the Illinois Central

thousands rode your rails from New Orleans
and parts of the rural South to Chicago
there were sharecroppers, blues and jazz musicians
and others...during the world wars they worked

in defense plants and other factories
when peace came they were resented by
returning veterans for their willingness
to work for low wages...some employers

no longer would hire them because of their
color...now trapped in central cities they
encountered hostility...their music
and culture thrived...they were appreciated

by those who embraced their talents
their acceptance into mainstream
society has been gradual...and
ongoing...many who live near the tracks

on the south side have a constant
reminder of how their families arrived

they must wonder if life here really
is better than the one they left behind

60. Western Colorado Sojourn

frequent loud whistle
blasts somehow seemed more
pleasant than offensive

a steam engine rode
the narrow gauge track
through mountain passes

and tunnels stopping
only once for water
near one of the highest

snow covered peaks on
the route offering
cliffside views of rushing

streams and towering pines
where no highways ever
intruded into the

picturesque landscape
bringing yesterday
into the present

61. Esquimalt and Nanaimo

you are the last railway
left on the island

you once connected
Victoria with

charming small towns like
Lake Cowichan, Parksville

Qualicum Beach, Courtenay
and Port Alberni hauling

passengers and freight
your proud history

was humbled as roads
and highways enabled

easier access
to a once unspoiled

rugged wilderness
what happened in much

of North America
in the immediate

aftermath of world war
finally affected

you early in the
twenty-first century

62. Ode to the Canadian Pacific

you once provided one of the most
spectacular trips by rail in the world
your scenic Montreal to Vancouver
excursion crossed the Canadian
Rockies in Alberta and meandered

along the Fraser River and through
the Okanagan Valley further west
your Royal Hudson steam locomotive
that once transported the king and queen
of England now rests quietly in Squamish

today your modern diesel engines
log fewer miles than in the past
but still contribute substantially
to North American economies
and maintain a notable legacy

63. Falling Further Behind

high speed trains have operated
over much of western Europe,
China, Japan, and elsewhere for

decades...light rail in those countries
reduces urban congestion
there...and here? fossil fuel, airline

and auto lobbies guarantee
U. S. passenger service will
never have a chance...so traffic

stalls regularly on the ground
and in the air; how much longer
can this neglect be accepted?

64. An Afternoon at Barton Springs

it was her first time ever
on any kind of train
she sat on my lap
for much of the time

she seemed in a state of wonder
and genuinely happy
she could not have been more so
than the man holding her

the train that ran through the park
and along the water
is no longer there
the memory will last forever

World Geography

65. The Teacher

he was a high school social studies teacher
for many years he taught whatever no one
else on the faculty wanted to teach

his staples were American history,
government, geography of the U. S.,
and even history of Europe...when the

man who for years had offered a course on
contemporary social problems retired
unexpectedly a new project was born

his passion, however, was world geography
in his "spare" time, he would read about distant lands---
their landscapes, people, and major industries

this topic soon became his avocation
he tried time and time again to convince his
long time principal to allow him to

offer a course on the subject...his request
was repeatedly denied...sensing an
opportunity when a new principal

arrived, the persuasive effort was placed
in high gear...willing to make changes, the new
administrator was impressed with his

enthusiasm...the curriculum
addition had finally become a
reality...the new world geography

teacher had traveled a fair amount and

could draw on those experiences in his
latest teaching effort...he could also now

travel vicariously to places he
had only dreamed of visiting on his
limited salary...his intellectual
curiosity now had no limits

66. Small and Progressive

there are no mountains but
rolling hills are common
water everywhere
frequent gently rolling
fog...absence of harsh cold

known for democratic
institutions, income
equality, a free
press, racial tolerance
and inclusion, little
or no corruption, and
legal same sex marriage

e-participation
among highest in the
world, economy fueled
by agricultural
exports and renewable
energy...mild climate,
geographically
small, socially advanced
Uruguay surprises
many with quality
of life rankings that rival
places thought to be elite

67. Reforestation and its Aftermath

the greenest country in the world
boasts a wide variety of

wildlife and plants thanks largely to
its success in reversing past

deforestation...all of its
electricity comes from wind,

solar, and geothermal sources
bordered by the Caribbean

Sea and Pacific Ocean, its
year round tropical climate has

just two seasons: a dry summer
and wet winter...it is widely

known for affordable housing,
quality health care, near absence

of illiteracy, longstanding
political stability,

and an enviable standard
of living...its economic

growth is driven by tourism,
pharmaceuticals, and software

development…all attractive
targets for foreign investment

unlike neighboring Panama
and Nicaragua, it has

held peaceful free elections for
over seventy years…it is

also one of the few nations
in the world to have no standing

army…its top national
priorities for many years

have been education and
environmental protection:

goals that appear to complement
each other well in Costa Rica

68. Tikal

ruin of an ancient Mayan city found in
present day impoverished Guatemala
built with limestone on ridges rising above

swampy lowlands surrounded by tropical
rainforest with many unusual
animals and flora including gigantic

kapok, the sacred tree of the Maya
its long succession of rulers had names that
translated to Foliated Jaguar,

Animal Skull, and Dark Sun...the site consists
of thousands of structures including a
great plaza, temple-pyramids, and a

palace complex...jade, shell, and ceramic
ornaments, hieroglyphs, and altars with
nearby tombs all tell stories of the culture

reasons for the collapse of Tikal and
Mayan civilization in general
are shrouded in mystery...theories

include some combination of extended drought,
overpopulation, deforestation,
soil erosion, warfare, and shifting trade routes

descendants still thrive today in Yucatan
Mexico, in Guatemalan cities, and
in hamlets across Central America

69. Teotihuacan: Birthplace of the gods?

Aztec people believed the gods created
the universe at this site near present day
Mexico City...in the middle of the

first millennium it was the sixth largest
city in the world...multi-ethnic with
housing that suggests class differences

art on its murals has been compared to
the paintings of Renaissance Italy
obsidian art was also common and

a major source of wealth...obsidian
knives were often used in human sacrifice
rituals whose procedures included

decapitation, removal of hearts,
and live burial...internal unrest,
war, drought, famine, and malnutrition are

postulated to be factors causing
desertion...today archaeological
evidence has been threatened by urban sprawl

fragments of ancient pottery were found
after trucks dumped soil from a site where a new
gigantic Walmart store was being built

70. South Sudan

finally independent after years
of dominance and civil war only
to have murder and torture reemerge
can this inhumanity possibly
end now that an element of self rule
exists and religious extremists have

their own land mass to the north? and yet, new
rounds of strife persist...the geography
of the south includes tropical forests,
grassland, swamps, high altitude plateaus, a
major river passing through Juba, and
mountains bordering Uganda...although
wildlife populations have diminished,

many rare animal species such as
antelope and buffalo are intact
vast oil drilling and new development
threaten a fragile environment...the
highest infant mortality rate in
the world, high maternal mortality,

a high level of illiteracy,
water shortages, and refugees from
Darfur present major challenges for
this long troubled land...a crisis further
compounded by a diaspora of
some of its most talented people to
North America and Western Europe

71. The Tatra Mountains

part of the Carpathian range
in southern Poland...home to a
variety of mosses, lichen,

mountain pine, and potent winds
permanent residents are brown
bear, wolf, deer, wild boar, and chamois

its waters are filled with brown trout
and alpine bullhead...at its
foothills sits Zakopane

a town rich in history and
known for its architecture,
cuisine, traditional dress,

and notable visitors
its highest peak Rysy covered
with snow year round lies on the

border with Slovakia
the majestic natural
beauty of these mountains has

overseen a rare blend of
lengthy tranquility and
harsh wartime tribulation

72. Cradle of Civilization?

it was more civilized then than now
people settled where the Tigris and
Euphrates joined...times were challenging
disputes no doubt arose...there was no
mass killing because differences

in the concept of a deity
existed...flooding was a frequent
threat...drought as well...people persevered
bound together...eventually
thrived...civility would last until.......?

73. Multiple Cradles

scholars tell us there were probably six
in such diverse places as present day
Egypt, Iraq, Africa, Mexico,
Peru and China...soon there were crops raised

in fields, livestock, cities, written language
and social institutions...not one of
these places was located in what would
become Europe or North America

74. Whither Greenland...and the World?

among the reindeer and arctic fox
between forests of gray-leaf willow
and white birch, both inside and outside
of the world's largest national park

above waters that house various
species of whale, during punishing
winters and frigid summers, it is
almost as if, on their way to land

masses further south, the glaciers stopped
here...for decades now, more moderate
air has been fighting back...as ice sheets
melt, new islands--masses of ground and

rock--are discovered...if the Greenland
ice sheet were to melt entirely, sea
levels around the world would rise by
over twenty feet...here and elsewhere

near the polar caps, the vanishing
glaciers send a sober warning, a
message that could prove especially
devastating to coastal cities

75. A Warming World

scientific forecasts predict
global warming to accelerate
and become most severe in
equatorial regions of
Africa, South America, and

South Asia but also harsh
in southern North America
and northern Australia
less rain and longer droughts are
devastating the farmlands of

Guatemala, hotter nights in
Nigeria are making it
easier for mosquitos
to breed, and in the U. S.
heat now kills more of the elderly

than all other weather events
including hurricanes combined
once again experts recommend
reducing combustion from
fossil fuels, making cooling

devices more accessible
and planting trees especially
near cities...in short, doing
everything differently
is anyone listening this time?

76. Parting Waters

in County Wicklow just south of Dublin
the waters meet to form the Avoca
a name borrowed from a river described

by Ptolemy...immortalized in the
early nineteenth century poetry
of Thomas Moore...far more beautiful than

his long ago depiction yet tainted
by long term industrial waste from a
copper mine and fertilizer plant...in

this garden spot of Ireland life goes on
a microcosm of a world filled with
memories of a serene unspoiled past

77. National Palace Museum

housing eight thousand years of rare art
some pieces from the collections of
ancient emperors...moved to Taipei
from Beijing when it was threatened by
the Japanese army and later
by the troops of Mao...diverse items
include paintings, carvings of jade and

ivory, calligraphy, bronzes,
porcelain, ceramics, agate, rare
books and documents, even ancient
musical instruments…miniature
pieces are the most impressive on
site...many locals call the combined
works one of the wonders of the world

78. The Urals

extending from the Arctic Ocean
southward into Kazakhstan
the conventional boundary
between Europe and Asia
resting upon layers of limestone,

dolomite, and sandstone...well endowed
with ores including gold, platinum,
nickel and chromite and such precious
stones as emerald, diamond, jasper,
and amethyst...point of origin

for multiple rivers that flow far
into both continents and home to
numerous lakes known to contain
medicinal properties...flora
of mountain clover, willow, and

poplar along with multiple
varieties of fauna have been
threatened by plutonium
producing facilities that have
dumped unfiltered radioactive

waste into some lakes and rivers
ongoing industrial
accidents have been common
amid token clean up efforts
and nominal regulatory

gestures, plutonium production
continues apace...the long time
and still geographically
striking wilderness area now has
a lengthy history of scars

79. Kashmir

invaders made the region
their colony and treated
their subjects poorly

after the world war
independence was finally
reluctantly granted

on the northwest border
of India the country
was known as Pakistan

an acronym for the
ethnicities of those
who reside there: Punjabi,

Afghani, Kashmiri,
Iranian, and Sindhi
Kashmir remains a disputed

area with portions lying
in India, Pakistan
and China...skirmishes and

outright warfare have been common
for decades...religious and
ethnic custom differences

are paramount...all three current
occupiers have nuclear
weapons...the world watches anxiously

North American Small Towns

80. Cross Village

the long descent from the Mackinac bridge concludes
lush green fields arise adjacent to the road that
parallels Lake Michigan's majestic shoreline
for the next several miles mild hunger beckons

at last a tiny hamlet with just four buildings
appears...one is a Polish restaurant that rests
on a bluff overlooking the water below
its fare rivals any in distant Chicago

its long list of authentic brews is supplied by
an exporter based in faraway Gdynia
has the word *oasis* been duly redefined?
as the journey resumes southward a trail of trees

before long encircles the narrow quiet road
occasional glimpses of the lake can be seen
from an elevated secluded vantage point
hopefully no large city will emerge for hours

81. Where a War Relic Quietly Rests

scenic country roads approach from four sides
a cobblestone main street is lined with small shops
now just another retail store an old train station
once witnessed passengers as they journeyed

from the east coast to the great lakes and points beyond
at the turn of the century a U. S. president
stepped from a train's coach to dedicate a canon
captured during the Spanish American war

as reporters from three states flocked to the scene
they missed on a beach just miles away the take off
of a flying machine three years before
a similar feat in celebrated Kitty Hawk

the three oak trees for which the town is named are no
longer there...the canon still sits inconspicuously
not far from where theatre patrons gather
and where frequent bicycle races are held

82. A Central Texas Tarnishing Gem?

your town square could have been the
set for *Back to the Future*
Victorian houses line several streets

history is evident in your antique stores
county courthouse and old time barber shop
an old movie house still features...old movies

ideas among locals are a
mixture of modern and very old
your small liberal arts college once

aspired to greatness until mismanagement
squandered some of its endowment
a quaint demeanor is in danger

of being swallowed up by a
vastly expanding nearby metro area
weekend traffic is now common

does enough of a small town feel remain
or will Georgetown become merely
another neighborhood in another suburb?

83. Stratford

on the way to Toronto
we stopped at a small town
people strolled the streets in

Shakespearean garb
live performances
would occur within hours

three story buildings were common
city hall and other structures
exhibited stunning architecture

English, Irish, Scottish, and German
ancestry were much in evidence
in sidewalk conversations

restaurants, and historical sites
we arrived just days before
a music festival would begin

rich in history and filled with
big name modern artists
we decided to maybe spend the night

we stayed for five nights
we left enriched culturally
we never made it to Toronto

84. Jasper

known for Banff and Lake Louise
Alberta possesses other treasures
just north of its rapidly vanishing glaciers
lies a town that will never grow large
because it lies entirely
within a national park
a railroad center surrounded

by mountains and glacier lakes
it is an ultimate getaway
less than fully discovered
void of luxurious hotels and spas
yet filled with quiet neighborhoods
inexpensive accommodations
and raw natural vistas

a skytram allows you to see it all
from near the top of a mountain summit
too high for trees to grow and much colder
than the river valley on which the town sits
forceful Athabasca Falls releases
its potent flow just south of town
completing its unique mix of unspoiled nature

85. Whidbey Island Escape

located within the rain shadow of the
Olympic mountains the community of
Coupeville is shielded from the rainfall that
regularly inundates most of western
Washington...rich in history its longtime
locally owned waterfront shops attract those
seeking rest after long sojourns on its

picturesque hiking trails...its proximity to
Canada lends an international feel
it is easy to lose oneself within
its many art galleries or wooded
forests where yearning for a return to
normal routine can be placed on hold for
the moment........or perhaps indefinitely

86. Southern Diversity

considered by many to be the birthplace of
baseball spring training, your young athletes who
would later achieve stardom included
Honus Wagner, Babe Ruth, Jackie Robinson, and

Hank Aaron...water temperatures exhibit
a huge range from cool lakes and streams to hot
calming baths fed from underground...fine arts
especially jazz and blues along with film thrive

few small towns feature picturesque botanical
gardens plus alligators, emus, and llamas
in your distant past gangsters proudly pranced along
your sidewalks undisturbed by what then passed for law

for decades a gambling mecca, your visitors
today are more mainstream: a mixture of
well to do who come a great distance and
nearby families of varied backgrounds

a future president lived here as a young boy
foothills peer upon your stately architecture
guests inside those buildings and outside stare back
and take in a setting unique to Arkansas

87. What's So Special About Clovis?

you are a bustling small town
surrounded by farms and ranches
your history goes back thousands
of years when early settlers to
the area left distinctive

sharp tools recently discovered
near the site of the present town
your modern history began
when railroads first came seeking a
stopover on their westward route

music was vital in your more
recent past when upcoming stars
like Roy Orbison and Buddy
Holly recorded some of their
first songs at a local studio

a decade earlier the elegant
Hotel Clovis ballroom hosted
the likes of Louis Armstrong
Tommy Dorsey and Glenn Miller
some would regard your scene today

as quieter despite its
annual music festival
concerts and rodeos...freight trains
have replaced passenger traffic
you are less trendy than the state's

more popular vacation sites
like Santa Fe or Taos and
less other worldly than rumored
alien landing site Roswell
you remain a western style

oasis in a region devoid
of big cities...you are a welcome
laid back community in a
climate where it seldom rains or snows
you are on the edge of the famed

multi-state Ogallala
Aquifer and near the middle
of a geographic mesa
known for its dearth of trees and bushes
your nighttime clear skies are spectacular

88. Wisconsin Island

as the ferry decelerates
the shoreline becomes visible
soon there will be lavender fields

and abundant foliage embraced
by a soft persistent breeze
once on shore a walk along

any beach offers a serenity
lacking on the nearby mainland
waves from Lake Michigan provide

captivating rhythmic sounds
with barely seven hundred
year round residents, a distinctive

small town environment enhances
the Washington Island landscape
economist Thorstein Veblen

spent many summers here where he
built a cabin for his wife and
stepdaughters...the cabin survives

one has to wonder how
inspirational he found the
setting and how many of his

ideas were born here
the ferry departs with
new writers amply armed

89. Across the River From the Old South

water is plentiful in this
old riverboat town where the
Muskingum River and Duck Creek
flow into the Ohio River
overlooked by early railroads

and highways, Marietta
still feels off the beaten path
its ancient ruins draw the curious
oldest town in the state, it was
home to abolitionists

and an important underground
railroad station during the
era of slavery...today
people enjoy its water
lifestyle and proud history

90. Clark's Point of View

originally home
to the Tillamook tribe
later visited by

Sacagawea with
her colleagues...all must have
marveled as tourists and

locals do today at
Haystack Rock protruding
just offshore...the town of

Cannon Beach retains its
pristine feel in part due
to a ban on retail

and fast food chains, instead
artisans have flourished
rolling white waves and dark

green hillsides spellbinding
in natural splendor
inspire pause, reflection

relaxed mind and body
redefine climatic
perfection...remind the

casual passerby
that a rapid pace need
not be of the essence

91. The Monterey Peninsula

we lived there for more than three years
our daughter was born in Carmel
we worked in Monterey and our

home in Carmel Valley Village
sat on a slope of the Santa
Lucia foothills...memories

are many...our fondest include
watching the fog roll into the
valley but stopping before it

reached the village, hiking in the
wilderness, strolling down Ocean
Avenue, fires in the fireplace

in July, spending a day in
Big Sur or Santa Cruz, watching
the waves in Pacific Grove, the

occasional night out at a
fabulous restaurant, sipping
wine while perusing books at the

Thunderbird Bookstore, and buying
vegetables at the farmers
market in nearby Seaside...it

was fairly brief...reality
beckoned elsewhere...experience
was beyond unforgettable

Gazing at the Stars

92. Trappist-1

housed in the faraway
constellation Aquarius
a red dwarf star is orbited
by seven earth like planets

where water and rocks
are highly likely
on at least some of them
it is billions of years older

than our own solar system
certainly long enough for
various life forms to evolve
the planets are close enough

together that travel
between them would be
relatively easy
is this where astronomers

are most likely to find
intelligent life?
has intelligent life there
already found us?

93. Chaco Canyon

ancient Pueblo hieroglyphics
of flowers, birds, and animals

mixed with similar drawings of
rocket ships and men in spacesuits

some scientists believe all of
this art is hundreds of years old

some possible explanations…….?

as children, we were taught
there were just nine planets
today we know there are
billions of galaxies

lakes on moons of Saturn
whose rings are slowly but
surely vanishing and
heat generated by

the interiors of
Uranus and Pluto
we are on the verge of
proving human life could

survive elsewhere if the
environment on earth
deteriorated
what yet additional

wonders still await our
discovery? is the
high probability
of intelligent life

elsewhere not worth efforts
to continue pursuit
of all cosmic wonders?
are those who deny the

benefits of science
merely fearful that the
folly of rapacious
lifestyles will be exposed?

95. Panspermia

microscopic life forms
trapped in debris
launched into space

after celestial bodies collide
asteroids comets and meteors
transport dormant living organisms

to new environments where
they can revive and colonize
what remains to be seen is

whether they will spread
powerful new sources of nutrition
or merely new diseases

96. Sirius

poets have long been drawn to the brightest
constellation in our sky...Hesiod Homer
Milton Dante Chaucer Voltaire Tennyson
Whitman and Dryden have all penned verse with
references to Sirius...ancient
mythologies across the globe have ascribed
magical powers to the timing of its

appearance and movement...astronomers
since Ptolemy have studied its unique features
yet have been unable to explain its change
from a reddish to blueish color...
despite its proximity to earth, its
brightness varies never outshining Jupiter
and Venus while at times fainter than Mars

and Mercury...we know Sirius is
slowly moving toward us and will become
brighter over the next sixty millennia
after which it will begin to drift away
chances to observe its features more closely
with advanced telescopes greatly enhance
prospects for scientific discovery

97. Is There Life on Moons in Our Solar System?

microbe life on planets other than Mars
is unlikely but might their satellites

house primitive life forms? four of the moons
of Jupiter and three of Saturn are

possible candidates...Europa is
known to have a huge subsurface ocean

frequent geologic activity
likely more water and oxygen than

earth...Callisto has tidal forces that
heat its subsurface ocean while Io

has more volcanos than anywhere else
in the solar system...even traces

of an atmosphere...the below surface
oceans on Ganymede contain salt water

Saturn's Titan has atmosphere similar
to that of early prehistoric earth

along with lakes, volcanos, plus methane
rain and snow...Enceladus and Dione

both have oceans below their surfaces
as do Neptune's Triton and Pluto's Charon

imagine the sea creatures that might emerge
from these little known cold distant places

98. Theia

over four billion years ago a
planet the size of Mars orbited
the sun at a safe distance from earth
when gravity disruptions occurred

on Venus this planet was vaulted
into a collision course with the
young earth...on impact debris from both
planets was hurled outward at some point

coalescing to form what we now
know as the moon...many scientists
believe much of earth's water came
from this planet...others theorize

that a more potent direct impact
would have destroyed both planets leaving
a mere asteroid belt between Mars
and Venus...asteroids today are

known to appear in fixed orbits that
occasionally come close to earth
it is not hard to imagine what
a second giant impact might do

99. The Colony on Mars

when humans first set foot on Mars
after a near eight month journey,
what will it be like? will they be
able to construct livable

habitats? withstand the cold and
dust storms? find a reliable
source of water? grow food? avoid
yet to be discovered unknown

illnesses? communicate with
earth? after these now seemingly
insurmountable hurdles are
conquered, will colonists agree

it was worth the risks? will crises
on earth have necessitated
perilous migration to a
second world? what will it be like?

Epilogue

100. The Winding Road

you were only six miles long
our farm was equidistant
from your two humble endpoints
because of all the German
immigrants who settled there

you were originally
simply called Germany Road;
during the Great War, flags waved
as you were renamed for the
sitting wartime president

many who later rode on
Wilson Road were unaware
how your name came about
when the interstate was built
you were important enough

to have a bridge over the
busy thoroughfare but not
so critical to deserve
your own entry and exit
today most of your farms are

gone, replaced by newer homes
on one and two acre lots,
by two gas stations, by a
lumber yard, by a tavern,
and even by a gambling

casino...you continue
to wind over rolling hills
and through fields now overrun
by trees, brush, and random weeds
you are still just six miles long